What I Eat

For Eliza

What I Eat

Christopher Wormell

Dial Books for Young Readers

New  York

donkey

hay

squirrel

acorns

mouse

cheese

chicken

seed

panda

bamboo

duck

bread

rabbit

carrot

COW

grass

seal

fish

parrot

nuts

elephant

leaves

butterfly

flower nectar

tortoise

vegetables

wasp

jelly

First published in the United States 1996 by
Dial Books for Young Readers
A Division of Penguin Books USA Inc.
375 Hudson Street
New York, New York 10014
Published in Great Britain 1996 by
Jonathan Cape, Random House
Copyright © 1996 by Christopher Wormell
All rights reserved
Printed in Hong Kong
First Edition
1 3 5 7 9 10 8 6 4 2

Library of Congress Catalog Card Number: 95-47655

The art for this book was created from handcut linoleum block
prints. Four blocks were cut for each picture. Each block was inked
with a roller and printed separately by hand, producing the black images
and the color areas. In certain instances, to achieve a shading or blending
of colors, more than one color ink was applied to the same block. All of
the art was color-separated by scanner and reproduced in full color.